Story Time with Signs & Rhymes

The Nest Where I Like to Rest
Sign Language for Animals

by Dawn Babb Prochovnic
illustrated by Stephanie Bauer

Content Consultant:
William Vicars, EdD, Director of Lifeprint Institute
and Associate Professor, ASL & Deaf Studies
California State University, Sacramento

visit us at www.abdopublishing.com

For Sam, who brings me tea and tends to the nest when I settle down to write—DP
For Cousin Mayella—SB

Published by Magic Wagon, a division of the ABDO Group, 8000 West 78th Street, Edina, Minnesota 55439.
Copyright © 2010 by Abdo Consulting Group, Inc. International copyrights reserved in all countries. All rights
reserved. No part of this book may be reproduced in any form without written permission from the publisher.
Looking Glass Library™ is a trademark and logo of Magic Wagon.

Printed in the United States.

PRINTED ON RECYCLED PAPER

Written by Dawn Babb Prochovnic
Illustrations by Stephanie Bauer
Edited by Stephanie Hedlund and Rochelle Baltzer
Cover and Interior layout and design by Neil Klinepier

Story Time with Signs & Rhymes provides an introduction to ASL vocabulary through stories that are written and
structured in English. ASL is a separate language with its own structure. Just as there are personal and regional
variations in spoken and written languages, there are similar variations in sign language.

Library of Congress Cataloging-in-Publication Data

Prochovnic, Dawn Babb.
  The nest where I like to rest : sign language for animals / by Dawn Babb Prochovnic ; illustrated by Stephanie Bauer ;
content consultant, William Vicars.
      p. cm. -- (Story time with signs & rhymes)
  Includes "alphabet handshapes;" American Sign Language glossary, fun facts, and activities; further reading and web
sites.
  ISBN 978-1-60270-670-5
  [1. Stories in rhyme. 2. Birds--Nests--Fiction. 3. Animals--Fiction. 4. American Sign Language. 5. Vocabulary.] I.
Bauer, Stephanie, ill. II. Title.
  PZ8.3.P93654Nes 2009
  [E]--dc22
                                                                                      2009002402

Alphabet Handshapes

American Sign Language (ASL) is a visual language that uses handshapes, movements, and facial expressions. Sometimes people spell English words by making the handshape for each letter in the word they want to sign. This is called fingerspelling. The pictures below show the handshapes for each letter in the manual alphabet.

This is the **nest** where I like to rest.

nest

These are the **eggs** I carefully laid to hatch in the nest where I like to rest.

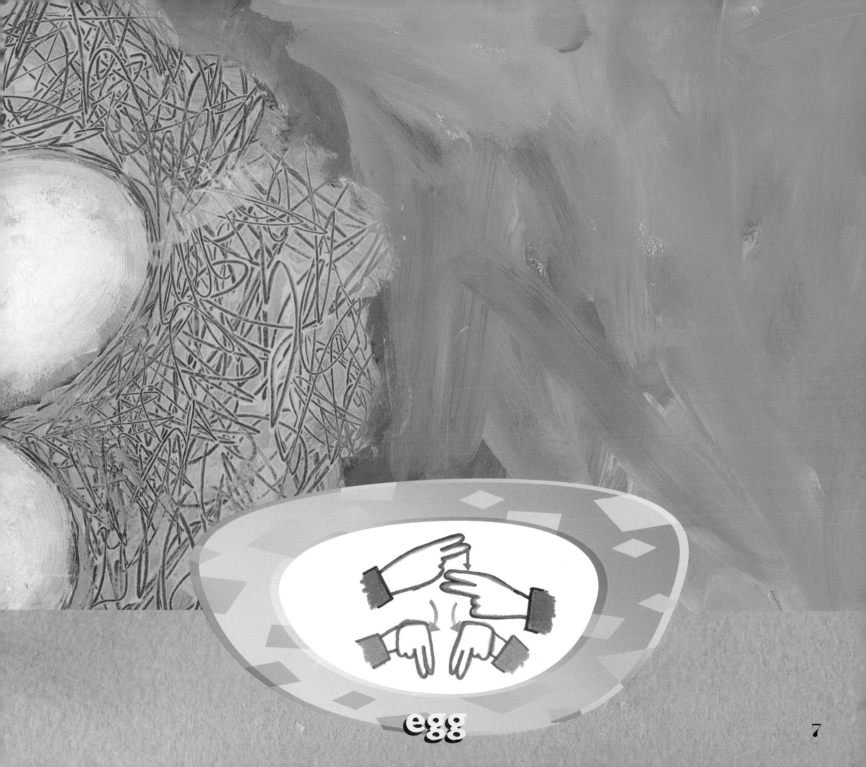

egg

This is the **rat** with a belly so fat that sniffed at the eggs I carefully laid to hatch in the nest where I like to rest.

rat

9

But how can **I rest** with a rat near my nest?

rest

This is the **cat** that spied the rat that sniffed at the eggs I carefully laid to hatch in the nest where I like to rest.

cat

This is the **goose** that somehow got loose. It honked at the cat that spied the rat that sniffed at the eggs I carefully laid to hatch in the nest where I like to rest.

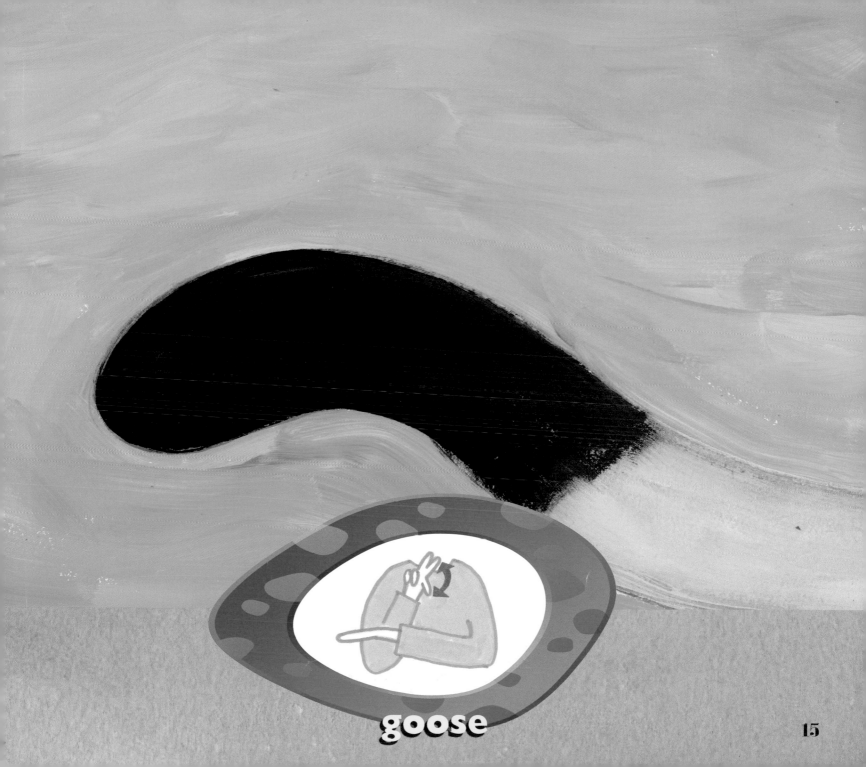

goose

Along came a **boy** named Mathew McCoy who called for the goose that somehow got loose. It honked at the cat that spied the rat that sniffed at the eggs I carefully laid to hatch in the nest where I like to rest.

16

boy

17

The goose kept on honking. The cat ran away.

The rat kept on sniffing. The boy shouted, "Hey!"

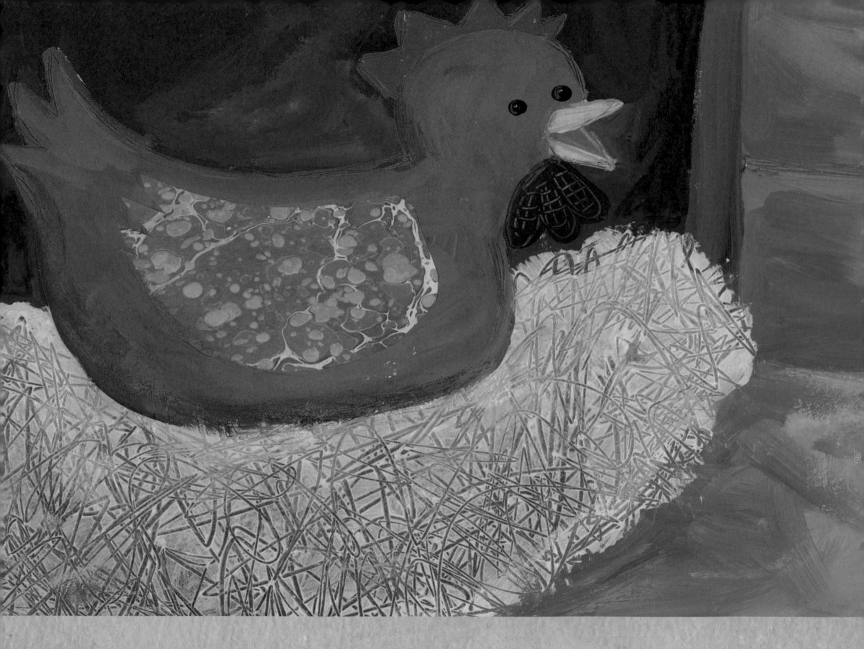

The rat finally ran. Good riddance you pest! But what was that ruckus inside of my **nest**?

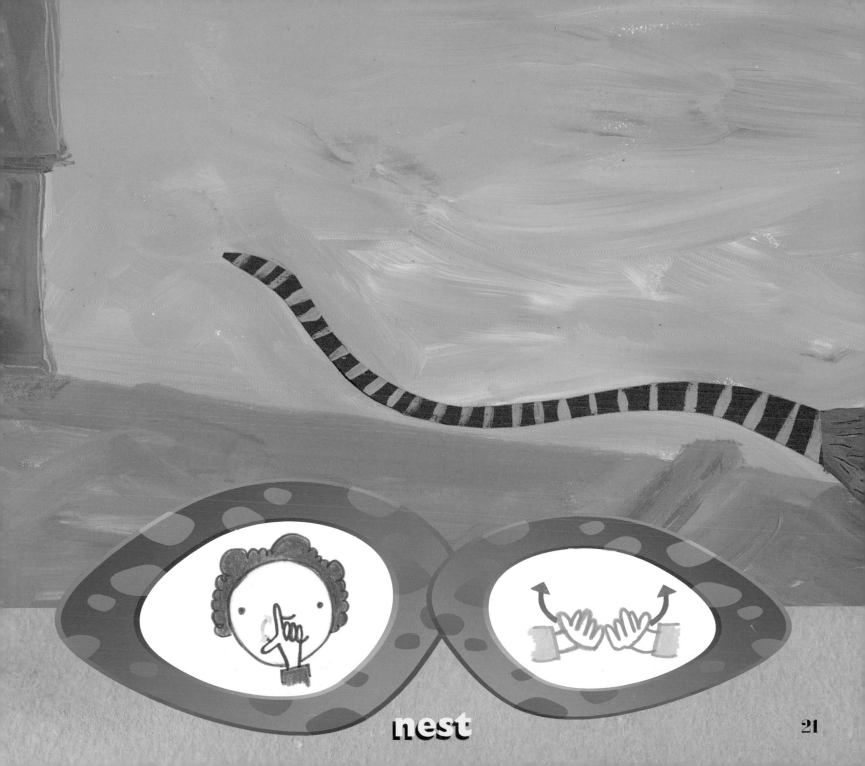

nest

I felt a sharp peck. So I did a quick check. I saw my new **chicks**. I counted all six.

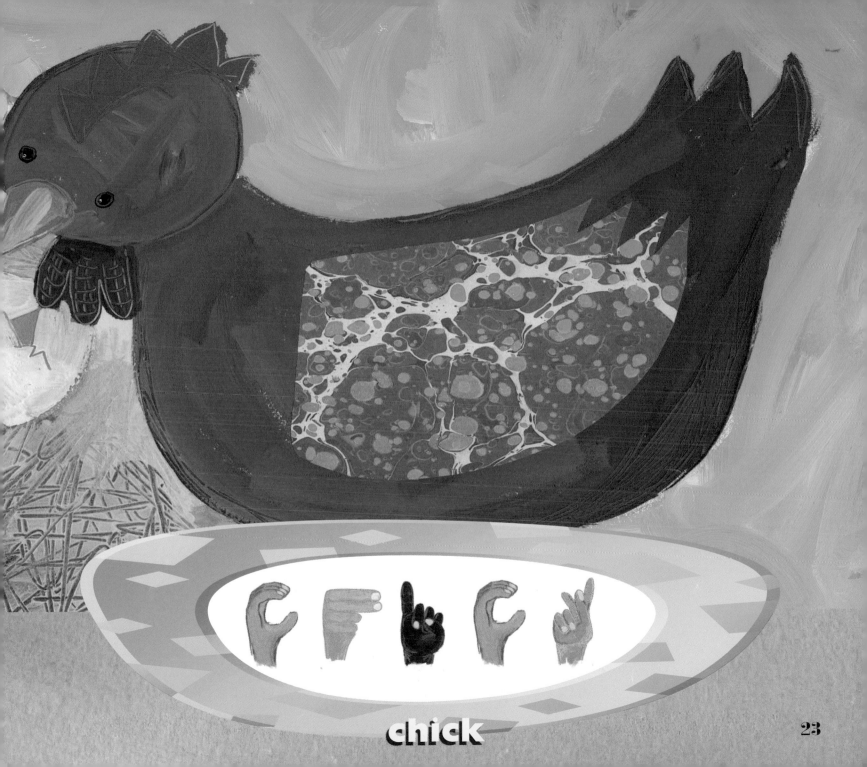

chick

The **boy** was excited. Of course, I'm delighted. My eggs are all hatched. They didn't get snatched.

boy

But how can I rest with these **chicks** in my nest?

chick

American Sign Language Glossary

baby: Hold both of your arms in front of your body and rock them gently back and forth like you are holding a baby.

bird: Point your "G Hand" in front of your mouth and open and close your pointer finger and your thumb two times. It should look like you are showing a bird opening and closing its beak.

boy: Tap your fingers to your thumb near the top of your head. It should look like you are touching the brim of a baseball cap.

cat: Move your "F Hand" from the side of your mouth and out. It should look like you are making cat whiskers.

chick: Fingerspell C-H-I-C-K. Or you can make the sign for "baby" and then "bird."

egg: Cross your "H Hands" in front of your body, then bring them out and away from each other. It should look like you're cracking an egg into a bowl that's in front of you.

goose: Hold your left arm in front of your body with your palm facing down. Lean your right arm on your left wrist, then open and close the first two fingers and thumb of your right hand two times. It should look like you are showing a goose with a long neck opening and closing its bill.

nest: Sign "bird" then sign "bowl" by holding your curved hands together in front of your body with your palms facing up. Now move your hands out and up. It should look like you are outlining the shape of a bowl.

rat: Gently brush your "R Hand" across the tip of your nose twice. It should look like you are showing the twitchy nose of a rat. This sign is similar to "mouse."

rest: Cross your open hands over your chest and drop your shoulders. It should look like you are taking a deep breath to show you are relaxed.

Fun Facts About ASL

If you know you are going to repeat a fingerspelled word during a conversation or story, you can fingerspell it the first time, then quickly show a related ASL sign to use when the word comes up again. For example, you can fingerspell C-H-I-C-K, then sign "bird" or "baby" then "bird." This shows your signing partner that you mean "chick" the next time you sign "bird" or "baby" then "bird."

Most sign language dictionaries describe how a sign looks for a right-handed signer. If you are left-handed, you would modify the instructions so the signs feel more comfortable to you. For example, to sign "goose," a left-handed signer would hold the right arm in front of the body and use the left arm to make the goose's long neck.

Some signs use the handshape for the letter the word begins with to make the sign. These are called initialized signs. One example of an initialized sign is the word *rat*!

Signing Activities

Create a Set of Flash Cards: Get some blank index cards. On the front of each card, write one word from the ASL glossary and draw a picture to go along with that word. You can also cut out pictures from magazines or old catalogs to illustrate the word. On the back of each card, write the hints you need from the glossary to help you remember how to make the sign for that particular word. Use your homemade flash cards to help you learn and practice new signs!

Sign of the Day: At the beginning of each day, post one of your homemade flash cards somewhere in your home or classroom where you will see it several times throughout the day. Each time you see the card, say the word out loud and do the sign. Once you can easily do the sign without peeking at the hints on the back of the card, you're ready to post and practice a new sign!

Sign of the Day Circle Game: This is a fun game for a classroom or a group of friends to play together. Begin by standing in a circle. Choose someone to be the first signer. The signer does their "sign of the day" from the activity above for the group. Those who think they know what word is being signed raise their hand. The signer calls on someone to say the word out loud. The first person to give the correct answer is the next signer, and the previous signer sits down. The game continues until no one is left standing up.

Additional Resources

Further Reading

Costello, Elaine, PhD. *Random House Webster's Concise American Sign Language Dictionary*. Bantam, 2002.

Heller, Lora. *Sign Language for Kids*. Sterling, 2004.

Sign2Me. *Pick Me Up! Fun Songs for Learning Signs* (A CD and Activity Guide). Northlight Communications, 2003.

Warner, Penny. *Signing Fun*. Gallaudet University Press, 2006.

Web Sites

To learn more about ASL, visit ABDO Group online at **www.abdopublishing.com**. Web sites about ASL are featured on our Book Links page. These links are routinely monitored and updated to provide the most current information available.